JANE KURTZ

FARAWAY HOME

Illustrated by E. B. Lewis

GULLIVER BOOKS
HARCOURT, INC.
San Diego   New York   London

Gulliver Books is a registered trademark of Harcourt, Inc.

Library of Congress Cataloging-in-Publication Data
Kurtz, Jane.
Faraway home/Jane Kurtz; illustrated by E. B. Lewis.
p.   cm.
"Gulliver Books."
Summary: Desta's father, who needs to return briefly to his Ethiopian homeland,
describes what it was like for him to grow up there.
[1. Ethiopia—Fiction.   2. Fathers and daughters—Fiction.   3. Afro-Americans—Fiction.]
I. Lewis, Earl B., ill.   II. Title.
PZ7.K9626Far   2000
[E]—dc21   96-47664
ISBN 0-15-200036-4

First edition
A C E F D B

Printed in Hong Kong

The illustrations in this book were done in watercolor on watercolor paper.
The display type was set in Herculanum.
The type was set in Columbus.
Color separations by Bright Arts Ltd., Hong Kong
Printed by South China Printing Company, Ltd., Hong Kong
This book was printed on totally chlorine-free Nymolla Matte Art paper.
Production supervision by Stanley Redfern
Designed by Linda Lockowitz

For my daughter, who always wanted to hear my stories about Ethiopia,
and for my Ethiopian friends whose real stories helped me write this book
—J. K.

For my friend Michael Bryant
—E. B. L.

WHEN DESTA dances into her house after school, the first thing she sees is the green envelope. She traces the bright stamp with her finger.

"Your grandmother back home in Ethiopia is ill," her mother explains. "Your father needs to go home to be with her."

"Daddy is going to leave us?" Desta runs to her father's favorite chair and curls up in it.

When evening comes, soft as a curtain closing, Desta's father takes her in his arms. He tells her again that *desta* means "joy," and sings a haunting song full of words she doesn't know.

"Ethiopia is so far away," Desta says. "I don't want you to go."

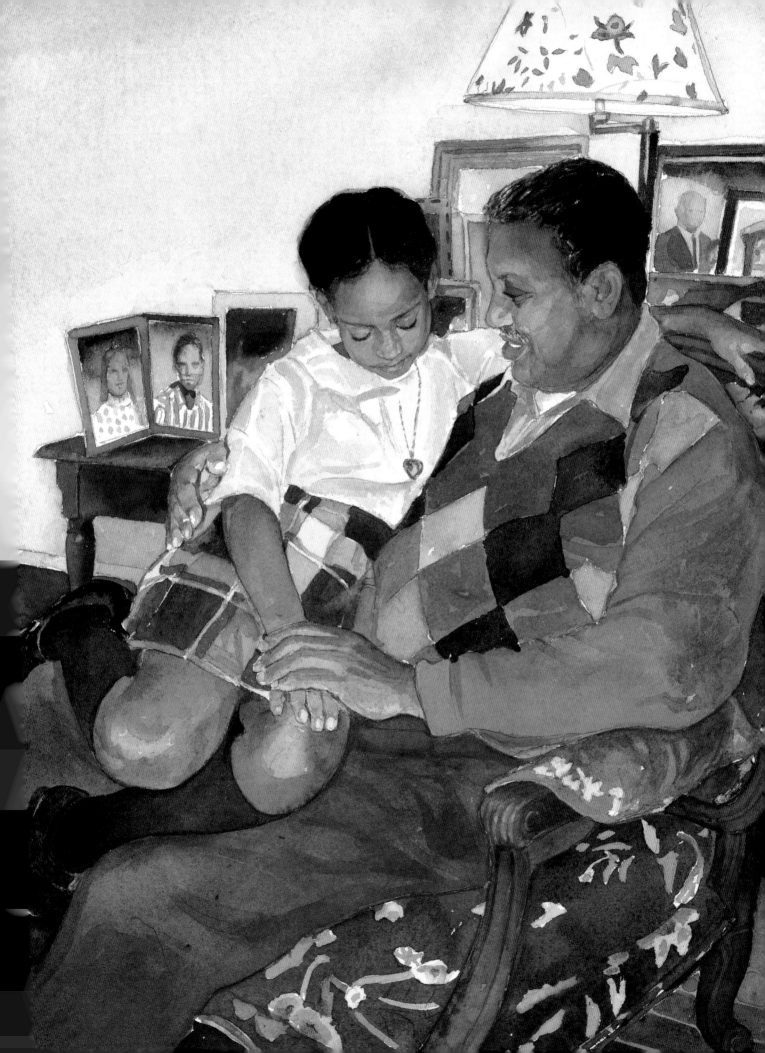

"For me, Ethiopia is never far away," her father says.
"Close your eyes and try to see green-gray mountains.
Think about a thick cloud of fog crawling up the valley
and the lonely sound of cowbells in the hills."
Desta closes her eyes and hears the wind chime
hanging from the front porch. *Do cowbells sound like that?*

"When I was your age," Desta's father says, "I carried grain on my head to the mill by the waterfall, where the grain was ground into flour. Then my mother made *injera* and cooked it over the fire that lived in a scooped-out place in the middle of the floor."

Desta shakes her head. In her home the fire stays in a fireplace. Her own mother cooks *injera* on the stove.

"My friend Christopher says Africa is hot," Desta tells her father.

He clicks his tongue. "Not where I lived. Sometimes at night the wind whooshed cold as old bones through the silver blue leaves of the eucalyptus trees outside my home. I slept on the floor wrapped in my *gabbi* to keep warm."

Desta tries to imagine sleeping on the floor and listening to silver blue eucalyptus. The tree *she* hears at night drops white blossoms on her bedroom windowsill, blossoms that look like snow.

"In Ethiopia," her father says in a faraway voice,
"hippos yawn from muddy pools and crocodiles arch
their backs above the river water. Shepherds pipe songs
of longing in the hills, and thousands of flamingos flap
in a pink cloud over the Great Rift Valley lakes. I wish
you could see the pink cloud."

"Did you walk to school like I do?" Desta asks.

"Yes," her father says. "And I carried a stick of purple sugarcane over my shoulder. Sometimes I couldn't wait for lunch but chewed out the sweet juices as I walked to school with mud squeezing up between my toes."

Desta stares at her father. "Why did you take your shoes off?"

He laughs. "I didn't wear shoes to school."

"Didn't wear shoes?" Desta thinks of the shoes in her closet—the black pair, the wonderful red pair, the new pair that she can hardly wait to wear. "No shoes," she says. "That's strange."

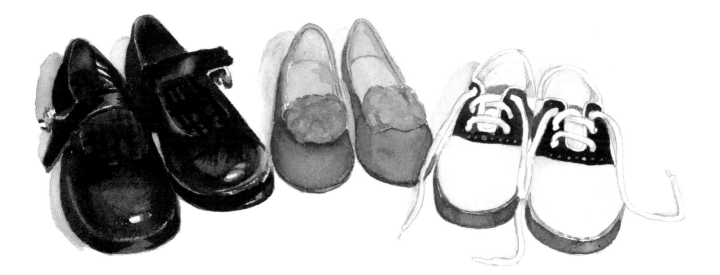

Desta's father gives her a mule ride to bed. He switches on her night-light and takes her hand in his. "Desta," he says, "my stomach is always hungry to go home. Now my *emayay* is very sick. It is time for me to go home and be with her for a while."

Desta thinks of hippos and crocodiles and a cold whooshing wind. "Daddy," she says, "would you like to take my night-light with you?"

"Thank you," her father says, "but my mother's home has no electricity. When I was a boy, sometimes the darkness pressed against me, and I heard the hyenas' strange coughing cry close by. But my *emayay* sang to me. She showed me that sunsets were bright borders on the cloth of the evening sky. The moon and stars burned holes in the cloth to light the night."

Desta looks out the window at the stars beyond the snow blossom tree. She shivers to think of the hyenas' cry. "Don't leave us to go there," she says. "Your home is too wild."

A sad look flies over her father's face, and before Desta goes to sleep, she hears him singing the haunting song with words she doesn't understand.

The next morning Desta walks to school, scuffing the toes of her shoes on the sidewalk. The wind chime rings in rhymes all the way down her block. Why does her father have to remember things like cowbells and silver blue eucalyptus? What if he goes away and never comes back?

Desta dreams all morning by the window. At lunchtime she asks Christopher, "Did you ever hear of anyone not wearing shoes to school?"

"No," he says. "That would be weird."

Desta frowns. When Christopher leaves, she opens her locket and looks at the face of the grandmother she has never met but whose picture she wears close to her heart. Her grandmother's eyes always look back at her, proud and strong. But is there also sadness glimmering in those eyes?

In the afternoon Desta looks up flamingos in the teacher's big book. As she studies their upside-down smiles, she thinks she almost hears the sound of a haunting lullaby somewhere at the edge of the classroom. After school she walks home barefoot, swinging her shoes, feeling the sun under her feet where it has soaked into the ground.

When evening comes, soft as a curtain closing, Desta climbs into her father's lap. "I think you miss your home a lot," she says.

"Yes, I do," her father says.

Desta sighs. "And your *emayay* misses you a lot."

"Yes," he says. "The same way I will miss you while I am gone."

"Will you tell me about your home every night until you leave?" Desta asks.

Her father holds her close. "Oh yes," he says. "And when I come back—and I *will* come back—I will have new stories to tell."

"Know what?" Desta says. "Shoes aren't so great."

Desta catches her father's smile and then closes her eyes. He will come back. Until he does, she can hold his stories in her heart.

As he sings to her, she sees a pink cloud of flamingos
rippling up from a dark blue lake, wrinkling the pale
cloth of the evening sky.

	DATE DUE		